CALL OF DUTY
UKRAINE

CALL OF DUTY
UKRAINE

By

AL Katar

ISBN 978-1-957956-56-5 (Paperback)
ISBN 978-1-957956-57-2 (Ebook)

Inquiries and Book Orders
should be addressed to:

Leavitt Peak Press
17901 Pioneer Blvd Ste L #298,
Artesia, California 90701
Phone #: 2092191548

CONTENTS

THE ATTACK

February 24th, 2022, A Grandmother enters a grocery store in the country of Ukraine, City of Kyiv. As she is buying tomatoes for a soup she is planning to prepare for her family.

She makes her way over to the butcher to buy some beef. She engages in conversation with the butcher. Butcher says, you think Putin will attack Ukraine; you know he has 100,000 plus troops on our northern border.

Grandmother says, I don't think so. I was born in Russia and lived in Ukraine for over 30 years.

I have relatives in Russia; that would be ridiculous for Putin to attack another Russian living in Ukraine; regardless of the politics that are in play.

The butcher says I hope you're right! I also have relatives back in Russia. Suddenly there is the sound of an air raid horn, and all of the people shopping in the store look at each other; as if they are cows looking at a new gate. Saying to themselves, I can't believe it "Boom"!

As the world governments scramble to make moves and policies regarding Russia invasion of Ukraine.

People in Ukraine or making life changing decisions by the minute. The war begun with no end in sight.

MARILYN WORLD

As the sun rises over the Great City of Baltimore, MD. Mrs. Marilyn the mother of two is going through a messy divorce and custody fight over her two kids.

The divorce does not go her way, and she also loses custody of her two kids, but is allowed visiting rights.

Mrs. Marilyn is employed at one of Baltimore City biggest hospitals as a registered nurse with many years of experience, especially treating gunshot wounds.

With her life in a tailspin, she watches the news on television of Ukrainian refugees', women and children being relocated around Europe, Canada and the United States. Even in her hometown of Baltimore MD.

Marilyn makes the decision to engage in humanitarian giving of her talent in the medical field.

She wants to serve in Ukraine as a nurse to help relieve the pain of others.

A few weeks later she says goodbye to her two kids, family, and friends. As she leaves for the airport in Baltimore for a flight first to England, Great Britain, and then to Poland.

Whereby she will cross the border from Poland to Ukraine.

FOREIGN FIGHTERS

On the flight to Poland, she noticed other volunteer fighters on the plane from all over the world looking to sign up with the Ukrainian military.

Sitting beside her there's a black man, 6 foot 3, 225 pounds with a British accent. He introduced himself to Marilyn as Mr. Rick. Marilyn says to him, what is a good-looking black man doing going to Ukraine. Mr. Rick says, what is a good-looking woman, black woman headed to Ukraine for lady.

Mr. Rick explains for the same reason you, and any other foreign fighters on this plane, is going for. To fight for freedom. Marilyn says I can respect that.

Two other foreign fighters on the plane interject themselves into the conversation. Hi, my name is Kelly from Texas, you can just call me Tx. HI, my name is Paul I 'am from Missouri, "The Show Me State".

Tx says, I see we are going to the same place to fight some Russians. I hope to bag a lot of Russians, because everything we do in Texas and Missouri, we do it big! The four make lots of small talk and become good friends.

After the plane lands in Poland, all the foreign fighters are placed on a train headed to the Ukrainian border.

At the border they are greeted by a Ukrainian military representative, and it is explained to all of them, that once you cross into Ukraine to join a military fight.

There is no going back until the Government of Ukraine gives you permission to leave. All of you, please think about it for a few minutes and give me your answers.

After a few minutes, all of the foreign fighters agreed to cross the border into Ukraine and face the unknown.

The foreign fighters are placed on trucks and driven away to parts unknowns. 10 hours later they arrive in Kiev, the Capital City of Ukraine.

There are destroy buildings all around them and the Ukrainian people they see, are in a panic mode of survival.

The foreign fighters are given instructions and placed on a number of trucks. Marilyn, Rick, Paul, and Tx attempt to get on the same truck but, are separated by a Ukrainian Sergeant, as they are placed on different trucks.

Marilyn says, where are we going? The Sergeant says, you will know when you get there, this is a need-to-know situation.

After a two-hour ride on bumpy dirt roads, they arrived at their destination.

Marilyn truck stops, but the other trucks Rick, Paul and Tx are on, continue to move to an undisclosed location. She wonders if she will ever see Rick, Paul and Tx ever again.

DOCTOR OLEK

Marilyn is a signed to the medical tent to treat Ukrainian and Russian wounded soldiers.

She is introduced to the Doctor officer named, Olek in charge of the medical unit. His pen name is "Doctor Feel Good" because he hands out pain pills. And at the beginning of their relationship, he is giving Marilyn a very hard time and little respect.

He is constantly all over Marilyn back, nerves and work performance. Marilyn strives to win him over with her skills as a nurse and do whatever is needed within the camp from hauling water, to cooking and making bandages out of bed sheets. But to no avail, the "Good Doctor" does not easy his resentment toward her.

She says to herself, maybe he's just prejudice against black women and black people, or he has some deep-rooted situation in his life; that he uses his anger to help cover that situation up.

I did not come to Ukraine to be abused. I could get that in the United States with my ex-husband. I'm here to do a job, to the best of my ability; I hope that will be enough.

After about a month at the medical tent there are wounded Ukrainian and Russian soldiers in recovery mode.

Some Ukrainian soldier's wounds will not permit them to be returned to the battlefield but go home to their loved ones.

The Russian soldiers on the Russian side of the tent are waiting to be sent back to Russia through a prisoner exchange program.

While changing and cleaning bedpans, a Russian soldier lying in his bed smoking a cigarette, says in broken English to her; my name is Captain Vaughn; thank you for taking care of us.

My leg wound is healing nicely. I look forward to returning to my tank unit in a few days.

The Russian soldier on my right was not so lucky, Peter is his name. He was my gunner in my tank unit.

His tank was hit by artillery, and he didn't get out in time. His face is a mess, can't see, can't talk. He just lies there and makes sounds.

We were told and sent to Ukraine to find and push out Nazi's. Many of my men have been killed and wounded.

And for all of what my soldiers have gone through, we have not seen one Nazi. Peter will be back home soon in Russia. The war is over for them.

Marilyn and Captain Vaughan make small talk as she continues her nursing duties. The Captain says to her, I'm hearing that the Ukrainian government and military have requested; that Ukrainian women return to their country, and train for combat duty and especially sniper training.

Marilyn says, I have not heard anything about that. I'm an American, so that is out of the question.

The next day buses arrive at the medical tent. The Russian soldiers are guided onto their bus for the prisoner exchange program.

Captain Vaughan expresses his sincere thanks to the hospital staff and to Marilyn for their kindness, as he takes his seat on the bus. The bus moves away, and Marilyn hopes he finds a safe journey.

As other wounded soldiers from both sides of the conflict continue to be brought to the medical unit. Marilyn is outside the tent evaluating and prioritizing the wounded to be treated.

As she makes her way back into the tent, the good doctor slaps her on her butt, backside as if she was some type of animal livestock.

She decides she's had enough of the good doctor and without thinking grabs a knife from a medical tray and puts the knife to the good doctors' throat and yells at him, I've had enough of you, you "Son of a Bitch"! Disrespecting me for what I do around here!

Either you stop treating me like an animal or I will due you, kill you right now!

The good doctor has no words for Marilyn, as he does not want to make body movements or say the wrong thing at this time. The other workers beg Marilyn to put down the knife, and let the good doctor go!

She calms down and slowly pull the knife away from his throat. I believe he got the message.

Unbeknownst to her at the same time from across the courtyard was a Ukrainian private soldier by the name of PyLyp.

He observed the whole knife incident and reported it to his platoon Sergeant by the name of Marko.

Sometime later that evening private PyLyp approached Marilyn and ask if she would meet with his Sergeant Marko. She agrees to the meeting.

As night falls on the encampment, Sergeant Marko introduces himself to Marilyn and says to her.

I heard what happened to you today. You have a great spirit about you, and I want you to consider joining my special combat unit.

We need a nurse to care for our wounded on the frontlines up north of Kyiv.

Another part of your duties; we hope to train you as a sniper. You have the right stuff to be trained for this type of job. Marilyn tells Sergeant Marko, I took an oath to preserve life, not take it.

Sergeant Marko explains, in this war I see it differently. You will be stopping another soldier that doesn't believe what you believe.

If that soldier is going to kill innocent women and children and you stop that soldier before the killing takes place; you will be preserving life and you would have not betrayed, your oath.

Later that evening while Marilyn is performing her duties to the wounded soldiers. She is called by Doctor Olek "feel good" to come into his private office.

The good doctor wants to apologize to Marilyn for his attitude and physical attack on her body. The doctor says thank you. For what you did today on setting me straight. I have a lot on my mind but, that is no excuse.

I'm feeling a lot of pain and loneliness because my wife and two young children a boy and girl were killed in our apartment at night. By a Russian guided missile.

I barely survived myself with bumps and bruises. It hit me hard that my immediate family is no more.

I deal with my emotions myself to much on my own. I must seek professional counseling concerning my emotions.

I realize I'm not the only man that has lost family and friends. I have the opportunity to re-build a new family and that's what I plan to do again.

I am sorry that I disrespected you; you're doing a great job, please forgive me! She accepts his apology.

Later that night Marilyn makes a cell phone call to her mother's home back in Baltimore. It being the weekend her two children should be at grandma's house.

The phone rings the line is picked up; hello her mother says. They make small talk concerning her two kids.

Both kids are placed on the phone call as they are very happy to hear from their mother. Marilyn is also overjoyed to hear their voices. She gives the kids instructions on how to behave and to do their homework.

Marilyn tells her mom that she has been given a promotion and she will tell her more about it, the next time they talk. The phone call ends.

NEW UNIT

Early the next morning Marilyn has packed her bags and joins her new unit as they prepare to leave for their base camp. After a two-hour ride through contested territory, they arrive at base camp.

Sergeant Marko introduces Marilyn to the special unit of troops. About 40 men soldiers, some 10 women soldiers are part of that make up.

Marilyn is also introduced to her new squad leader by the name of Alona, A female soldier.

Alona, explains the makeup of the unit. For every five men there is one sniper assigned to that group. There are six female snipers so far in this unit.

You will receive sniper training, but you still have to perform your medical duties on warrior soldiers on both sides if necessary. Those are your orders for now.

Marilyn is told to make herself comfortable in any of the burned-out apartment buildings that are nearby.

Alona, says she herself is on guard duty from 2:00 AM to 4:30 AM in the morning.

Your turn Marilyn, to be on guard duty will start tomorrow. Get something to eat and rest yourself for the night. But there are no guarantees out here. You're never really off duty.

You're on 24 hours a day that's the reality.

Later that evening Marilyn is given a warm welcome to the unit by other soldiers. Private PyLyp and his girlfriend fiancé, private Daryna are schedule to be married when the war is over. You can say they are man and wife sniper team.

They are glad to have a combat medic in their unit. Because a lot of their friends, fellow soldiers have died because they did not have a combat medic on the frontline.

Marilyn makes her way over to a burned-out apartment building; where the army unit kitchen is set up to get the meal of the day.

She sees that the cook there is a black man with a patch over his left eye.

She assumes that the injury was related to being in combat. Marilyn introduces herself to him, hello my name is Marilyn, what is your name brother?

He answers and says my name is Pete. I am the designated cook for this unit. I have been here for at least a month at this job.

Would you like a bowl of soup. This is all we have right now, I hope you'll enjoy it.

Our new food supplies have not arrived yet. But day to day, I have to scrounge and forage for food, so bona petite!

Marilyn says this is some good soup. Pete says you're just trying to be kind, but I appreciate the thought. The two find time to make small talk. Marilyn says to Pete that's a funny looking stove you're cooking on.

I've never seen that type of stove before, what is it called? It's called a "Barrow Stove "or combat stove. I can cook with three pots on top of it at the same time. I was told that some Military or Army guy invented it. They sent me the top portion.

It connects to the top of any oil barrel in the world. You just have to put some wood in it, or coals. I also use Russian soldiers' helmets, because of their shape, they make great cooking pots, so I can make helmet Stew.

We have plenty of wood around here from bombed out buildings, Schools, homes, and churches.

Thanks to Mr. Putin and the Russia people. The stove is not perfect, but it will do for now.

Marilyn understands that Pete is somewhat of a joker or comedian. His humor is needed in this war to keep us sane.

Pete says to Marilyn what brings you to Ukraine? Marilyn replies to him. My life had gone into a tailspin.

I guess, I'm running away from something or running to something! Trying to reconnect with my feelings.

Maryland says to Pete what brings you to Ukraine? Pete says I'm from Atlanta GA.

The pandemic shut down the restaurant I was working in as a cook.

Saw the war in Ukraine on television and saw there was a need for my cooking skills.

So, I joined "World Kitchen International" to help feed people. I was in Kyiv and met a Ukrainian girl and fell in love.

We worked side by side in the kitchen. One day without warning; a rocket missile hit our location and my girlfriend was killed. In the attack my left eye was damaged.

I had to place my girlfriend in an open grave with her in a plastic bag. After that, I felt I had an obligation to continue working in her memory.

Maybe I have Stockholm syndrome, they both laugh!

After dinner Marilyn lays down for the night on a mattress on the floor of a burned-out apartment building. Thinking about what is to come in the morning.

VILLAGE OF BUCHA

Early the next morning she is awakened by Alona. And she is told to pack up her things because they are headed to the town of Bucha, that the Ukrainian Army has taken back from the Russians. The unit loads up on trucks as they proceed north to the village.

Once they reach the outskirts of the town, they see a lot of combat vehicles blown up or disabled.

There are also a lot of automobiles and trucks that are destroyed or on fire. They disembarked from the trucks and have ordered to survey the town and to be aware of booby traps.

As they enter the village, they see dead men and women. Some with their hands tied behind their backs and shot in the back of their heads.

All of a sudden running out of one of the destroy houses is a little girl holding a doll, asking where her mother and father are? The soldiers have no answers!

Marilyn finds some civilians with minor flesh wounds, and she goes to work within her medical bag to help ease their pain.

Soon Marilyn realized she could only treat their outer wounds, not their inner wounds.

At this point other vehicles start to arrive in the village, carrying lots of journalists.

They take pictures and film of what has taken place in the village. The smell of the many dead bodies is very strong!

These Ukrainian civilians have been dead for at least 7 to 10 days. Marilyn assists in placing bodies in plastic bags and transporting them to a field where a large hole has been opened up in the earth.

Where the bodies are position side by side. Marilyn says, to herself where is the humanity in all of this she wonders! After six hours in the village of Bucha, they have done all that they can do for these people.

Marilyn unit has been ordered to move out to a new location in the eastern region of Ukraine; closer to the Russian border.

After traveling all night, they arrived at their new base camp. That morning Alona tells Marilyn it is time for sniper training.

They proceed to a wooded area and meet other female snipers in training. Marilyn notices the women have no hair on their heads. Alona explains hair is not necessary. That's one less thing a soldier has to worry about.

Alona explains that the Military and their President has asked that more females over the age of 21 return to Ukraine for military service.

The women you see here have recently returned as they have left their children with relatives. Enough talk let's get down to business.

Alona instructs Marilyn in the fine art of a sniper. I've been a sniper for about a year now. I will explain the do's and don'ts. Marilyn your first job as a sniper will be a sniper's helper or spotter.

The two of them find a good sniper position to practice their craft. Marilyn is given a pair of binoculars as they are both camouflaged.

A few targets have been placed in positions to be shot at.

Alona fires a few rounds and now it's Marilyn turn to fire. After a hard day of training, they return to base camp.

There Pete has just finished cooking up a large pot of beef Stew. Pete says, today we got fresh supplies from NATO, so dig in, hope you like it.

Pete, says to Maryland during dinner, you had fresh medical supplies come in also today. You need to fill your medical bag.

I hear you guys are going on the front line in the morning. You're going to need that medical bag filled to the top.

Pete says I hear Mr. Putin wants to go nuclear.

Marilyn says do you believe that? Pete says anything is possible. I like a little radiation flavoring in my soup. They both laugh!

ALONA WORLD

Later that evening Alona and Marilyn find time to make small talk. Marilyn asks her what her story is of being in this unit. She replies, I have a husband and two children a boy and a girl that were relocated to Poland.

My husband was a Ukrainian soldier that lost the use of his left arm. And because of that, he was able to leave the country with our children. It was my decision to stay behind and fulfill my family's obligation to defend our country.

I hope to reunite with them very soon. As soon as this war is over the better. Marilyn says to Alona, I see you walk with a limp. She responds, I have been shot in my left leg and I deal with the pain of it. Marilyn is told she has guard duty tonight from 1:00 am to 4 am. Turning in for the night.

Earlier next morning Marilyn and her unit are loaded onto trucks to move to the front line.

As they approach their new position, the sound of gunfire and artillery fire is becoming louder and louder the truck stops; and they are told to disembark and follow their individual squad leaders to take up positions.

Alona and Marilyn fine a suitable sniper position overlooking an open field. The trails of tracer bullets are in the air. Marilyn job at this time, is to use her binoculars to locate Russian soldiers and instruct Alona where to fire.

Maryland locates a soldier with a Russian Insignia and red color band on his arm.

Marilyn says to Alona do you see him to your left Alona replies yes, I'm taking the shot now. She fires her 7.62 rifle bullet and hits her target. The soldier falls down immediately.

Marilyn spots another soldier and again Alona fires and hits five out of seven of her targets with clean shots. The other two shots may have wounded the other soldiers.

The battle rages all morning and afternoon. Both sides Russian and Ukrainian soldiers are killed or wounded.

As the sun disappears over the horizon. The artillery fire and gunfire take a pause. All Ukrainian fighters are instructed to dig in, which means make yourself a foxhole.

The soldiers understand they must hold their positions through the night are until they are properly relieved of duty or replaced by other soldiers. After the two ladies finish digging their foxhole.

They break open their can rations and begin eating their dinner. Marilyn says cold beans again. Alona says put some of my hot sauce on them. I never come to the field without two things.

Hot sauce and liquor. I like the Deer Head and sometimes I get the Kentucky Bean. Marilyn says, where did you learn that? Alona says it's in the sniper's handbook, they both laugh!

Alona asks Maryland how she felt about that day's work. She says I really can't think about it. I have to delete it from my mind. Alona says tomorrow it won't be any better.

Marilyn says, what is that horrible smell? The wind is blowing our way.

Alona says the smell is from dead soldiers that have not been picked up and Buried on the battlefield. The sound of a wolf Pack cries out in the night, the wolves rule the night.

I will take the first guard duty for two hours and I will wake you for your turn.

As the sun rises the sound of artillery is in the air. Some shells fall within 100 meters of the ladies. Marilyn is ordered to go back to base camp, to care for the wounded. On arriving at base camp, she goes right to work.

Ukrainian and Russian soldiers are brought in for treatment. She is very busy attending to the soldiers. Some of the soldiers on the stretchers are already dead.

But she has to pull back the sheets covering their heads to make sure they are deceased. She pulls the sheet from over the head of one soldier and she is in shock at what she sees.

She recognizes the Russian soldier is Captain Vaughan. That she treated not long ago.

This time in combat; he didn't make it!

She replaces the sheet back over his body and continues her nursing duties. Later that evening she returns to her foxhole on the frontline.

The next day is more of the same. More shots fired, more death, more sorrow.

Marilyn is treating more and more soldiers. Ukrainians and Russians on the field of battle, die as they fall.

She is performing double duty as a sniper and field medic. The wounded cry out for pain killers, which is the number one drug on the battlefield.

For the next 10 straight days Marilyn unit undergoes combat day and night. To which a person forgets what day it is.

The Army unit relocate to a town that has been won back into the hands of Ukrainian soldiers. Because of the hard fighting, her unit has lost a number of soldiers both male and female.

The unit wants to enjoy a few days of relaxation before returning to the frontline.

Pete sees Marilyn disembarking from a transportation truck and greets her. Pete says he has the kitchen set up at the bombed-out school and dinner will be ready in a couple of hours.

Marilyn says has my medical supplies arrived. I'm out of everything, especially pain killers. I thought I had more in my bag.

I guess I used them all; it's been a busy week. Yes, Pete says I have them, see you at dinner. We're having helmet Stew.

As Marilyn enter Pete's kitchen area her heart jumps with joy as she sees an old friend. It's Rick the foreign fighter from England, Great Britain.

Rick jumps to his feet and they embrace one another with joy. Rick says, You're a site for sore eyes! I wonder what had happened to you.

They both sit down and enjoy their dinner with smiles on their faces. After dinner they bring each other up to date on what they have experienced, so far in the war.

Marilyn sees a few bumps and cuts on Ricks head and hand as, she treats him with fresh bandages.

Alona informs Marilyn she is going to make a "zoom" call to her husband and two kids in Poland. She is very excited about the opportunity to speak and see them on the computer screen.

Marilyn says whatever happened to Paul from Missouri and Tx from Texas. Rick says they were both in my combat unit. Paul was killed last week in combat. They shipped his body back home to Missouri; he was a good soldier.

Tx on the other hand was wounded and captured by the Russians. I heard he is alive, and they are using Tx on Russian television as a propaganda tool right now. He will probably be part of a prisoner exchange operation sometime in the future.

At this time Rick is called over to the side to talk to other soldiers. Alona walks over to Marilyn and they make woman talk.

PARTNER UP #1

Alona says, is that your boyfriend? She says no! Just a good friend. Do you have a girlfriend?

No, she says. Alona says, everyone in this war has choices to make or partner up. The next day is not promised to anyone.

As you can see around the compound here, soldiers are pairing up to "Make Love". You don't have to really know all things about your partner.

My partner for a while has been Angelina, Pete assistant cook.

Because we're all fighting for the same thing, freedom and to get back to our families and our way of life.

The partnerships help take away the stress of war. Just don't be judgmental; you will know when the time is right for you to partner up.

Marilyn looks across the courtyard and sees Rick engaged in conversation. The soldiers are discussing the new NATO fighting vehicle, a 17 ton lightly armored "Airborne Assault Tank", that is desperately needed on the battlefield.

There are two things a Russian soldier is terrified of. One, is a baby eating an ice cream cone. The second thing is another tank!

Suddenly a female soldier put her hand on Rick shoulder. They look Into each other's eyes and without saying a word they move off into the distance "To Make Love".

Marilyn absorbs what she was told and is receptive to the knowledge she has learned. Now she has to go on to guard duty for the rest of the night.

Early the next morning Marilyn is relieved an hour earlier than expected from guard duty.

As she enters her sleeping quarters, she encounters Alona going through her medical bag. What are you doing Alona? Alona says, I'm looking for pain medicine for my leg and I'm taking all of it this time, I need it!

Marilyn says put it back, you're just a drug addict, she refuses. A fight breaks out between them; it's a regular all-out catfight.

Other soldiers hear the mayhem and break up the fight. Sergeant Marko comes into the room and says, I don't know what the fight is all about, but you two, need and will control yourselves.

Get it together yourselves or I will get it together for you!

BETRAYAL

Later that day Marilyn goes into an abandoned building to relieve herself and while doing so, she hears a voice coming from another room.

She hesitates to investigate, but her curiosity gets the best of her. As she moves down a hallway, she looks through a hole in the wall and, sees Angelina on a cell phone talking to someone as if she is doing it secretly.

Marilyn Informs Alona and Alona informs her Sergeant Marko. Sergeant Marko informs the officer of the unit. The officer has Angelina arrested and her phone brought to him to investigate.

After the interrogation, it is determined that Angelina, is a spy for the Russian government and Army.

And she has been transmitting our Ukraine Army locations. Telling them for weeks and she was paid $10 a day to do so.

She was born in Ukraine, but her parents are Russians living in Russia. So, her loyalty has been a mixed bag.

All of the unit soldiers are upset and perplex about the situation. Sergeant Marko says to the officer; do you want to call the "USB" which stands for Ukrainian Security Bureau.

The officer explains to the soldiers they will discuss it and give them my answer in one hour. An hour passed, and they read the decision to the soldiers.

Because Angelina was born Ukraine, she is not granted normal protection as a "P.O.W" prisoner of war. It has been decided that she will be executed by a 12-person firing squad made up from this unit.

Marilyn says, to her Sergeant Marko, will I be part of the firing squad. No, he says! It must and has to be an all-Ukrainian unit. No international fighters can participate. We do not want an international incident.

Your job Marilyn is to cut 24 sticks to different links. So, the 12 soldiers that pull the shortest straws will be on the firing squad.

Marilyn completes her task, and all soldiers pull the straws. Alona pulls a long straw, but she trades her straw for a short straw to be part of the firing squad.

The officer says, Angelina will have one hour to make peace with her God. An hour has passed, and Angelina is place against a wall of a burnt-out apartment Building. Marilyn, Pete, and Rick are only witnesses to this event.

All bystanders including the mayor of the town and some townspeople are present with their hats in their hands. The 12-soldier firing squad faces Angelina.

She is offered a blindfold, but she refuses it. She is asked, if she has any last words. She says with her fist in the air, glory to Russia, glory to President Putin!

Officer, says ready, aim, suddenly a single shot Rings out! It is from Alona rifle only. Everyone is not so surprised. No one says a word, and everyone just walks away in silence.

The next day the Army unit moves to a new town and back on the front line of combat.

A few weeks have passed, and the memory of Angelina is fading away slowly but, never to forget. After a hard day of fighting the unit returns to base camp for a much-needed rest.

PARTNER UP #2

After eating a good dinner prepared by Pete. Marilyn Is walking back to her sleeping quarters.

Sergeant Marko intercepts Marilyn and starts giving her a hard time on what she didn't do right that day.

Suddenly Marilyn pulls out her pistol and pushes it into the sergeant's face; with anger on her face not saying a word. She pushes him into a side door of an apartment building.

Backed him into a room with little light; still holding the pistol to his head. She does not say a word, as if time is standing still for one minute.

She slowly removes the pistol from his neck and places it on a table.

They look into each other eyes and Marilyn reaches up and tears his shirt open and kisses him. Sergeant Marko responds in like manner removing each other clothing.

With intense Love making not under the best conditions. Sergeant Marko violently turns her around and bends her over the table. The rest is history.

The next morning Marilyn and Alona are walking toward a waiting truck to go back to the frontlines. Alona sees that there is something different about Marilyn body language.

She stops her and spins her around face to face; and says you did it, didn't you? Marilyn says let's get going, we don't want to be late.

As they are boarding the truck suddenly there is an explosion where the unit kitchen is. Marilyn says oh my "God" Pete. She jumps from the truck and rushes over to the kitchen. Pete is lying face down on the ground.

She says Pete, Pete are you all right. He turns over with the look of pain on his face and says I've been shot in the butt.

I got a piece of Putin missile in my butt, ASS! I guess you can say, I'm ASS out! Marilyn gives him a shot of pain medicine as the ambulance takes him away. She boards the truck looking straight ahead in silence, as the unit travels to the next combat mission.

LAST BATTLE

There is an intense battle raging; tracer bullets flying through the air, as if they were fireflies in the night. Alona platoon is taking heavy fire and casualties.

Marilyn is doing all she can to take care of the wounded soldiers. She is running from place to place to give care. She is told to go to a farmer's barn because there are wounded soldiers there. After entering the barn, she finds Rick and other soldiers.

Rick is wounded but still alive. He might just have a concussion because of his headwound. After treating the wounded there, she returns to the front line.

Alona sees one of her squad members get hit just feet away from a bombed outbuilding. Alona instructs Marilyn to cover her.

Alona crawls out from behind the wall on her belly to reach the wounded soldier.

She had little time to notice that she is being watched by a Russian sniper.

The Russian sniper being a professional at what he does understands; that he will use the wounded soldier that is in an open area; as bait for any Ukrainian soldier that wants to rescue the wounded soldier, he lays in wait.

Alona reaches that wounded soldier. The Russian sniper put Alona in his crosshairs. He fires from his camouflage position and misses her.

He then interjects another round into his rifle and adjust his fire, he fires once more and hits Alona in her left shoulder.

Alona collects herself as she is bleeding and drags the wounded soldier back toward the brick wall. Just before reaching the wall, Marilyn assists with the wounded soldier. The sniper fires once again and hits Alona; this time in her lower back.

The wounded soldier receives prompt medical assistance. Marilyn reaches into her medical bag to treat Alona wounds.

Alona tells Marilyn she's not going to make it. Alona sees Russian infantry closing in on their fragile position as they are out numbered. Alona does not want to be taken prisoner.

She instructs Marilyn, take out your pistol to due me! In other words, kill her.

Because she doesn't want to rely on the mercy or non-mercy of the Russians soldiers. Marilyn is in a state of conflict in her humanity.

Marilyn tries to convince Alona to take her chances with the Russians. At least She will have a chance of living as a P.O.W.

Alona, says to Marilyn, you knew before today as I warned you. You may have to do this deed, as I had to do it to my fellow Ukrainian soldier at one time.

I didn't want to do it, but my love for that soldier; I had to obey that soldier one last requests.

Now I'm asking you; I'm begging you to do me; kill me, it's your job. Marilyn humanity still has sway over her. She cannot bring herself to shoot her best friend.

As the enemy troops are getting closer to their position.

Suddenly Alona summons the strength in her right arm and slaps Marilyn across her face; and with a loud voice say, kill me, kill me now! The atmosphere between these two good friends is wearing thin!

Alona once again slaps Marilyn across the face and grabs a fist full of Marilyn shirt and pulls her close and kisses her.

And says shoot me now with a convincing voice of urgency.

Shoot me now! "You Black African American bitch"!

Marilyn mind is still in a fog, but she fires a single shot from her pistol to Alona forehead. And as if time stood still as Alona falls backwards onto a pile of broken concrete. Time is standing still.

Marilyn bends down over Alona and kisses her on her forehead.

Marilyn picks up Alona sniper rifle and for a moment forgetting her emotions and vacates the area. She does not look back, she soldiers on.

HOME GOING

Two weeks later the Ukraine, Russian conflict has halted, or a cease fire has taken place. Marilyn returns to her a sign military base. She is sitting alone at a table in a large airplane hangar. Other Ukrainian soldiers are all around her.

The atmosphere is electric, and people are very happy and sad at the same time. As they realize they have to confront the rebuilding of their country and their lives.

Her platoon Sergeant Marko is in the hangar handing out information to soldiers, as he sees Marilyn alone at her table. He says to her, I heard what happened to Alona.

We have all lost people that we have loved during the war, and we have lost them! Alona was a good soldier, the best. Take comfort she died, so her country citizens and family may live free.

Private PyLyp and Private Daryna are coming to the hangar and sees Marilyn at her table.

They are very happy to announce to Marilyn that they are getting married right away.

They ask Marilyn where is Alona? Marilyn is slow to speak, as the happy couple sees Alona sniper rifle on the table with the letter "A" cut into that wooden stock or butt of the rifle.

The couple both knew at that moment Alona was dead!

At this time Marilyn stood up from the table and adjusted her uniform and said to them both, she died. I killed her as she requested. This is what you're going to do for me.

You're going to take her sniper rifle and put it in a place of honor in your home above your fireplace, that's what you do.

And when I come back to visit your home, it better be there! I'm headed back to the United States. I hope I have been of service to the Ukraine people.

Goodbye you two, Marilyn, Marilyn a voice shouts out in the distance. Marilyn looks toward the sound of her name being said.

To her delight, it is Rick and with him is Tx. They all three embrace each other, with joy in their hearts.

Marilyn says to Rick how is your head? Rick says, when I saw you, the pain went away. Marilyn says to Tx, how is your leg? It's coming along.

The doctor says, I'll be fine in a couple of months. The Russians had to let me go.

They said I talk too much.

Suddenly an ambulance pulls up to the hangar and out of the back of it, a man steps out. It's Pete wearing a diaper. Pete says don't laugh at my diaper.

When you guys get older, you'll be wearing one too. The four amigos are together once again, minus one Paul.

As they all steps on a bus headed to the airport. Only time will heal Marilyn heart inside, that no one else can see of her love for Alona and the Ukrainian people.

The End

SYNOPSIS

Most wars are started when old men run
out of new ideas and stop dreaming.

There are many rules of war. And
the first two rules of war are.

Number one, young men and
women die. Rule #2, you can't
change rule #1, someone said.

Ukraine Female Snipers

By
AL Katar

UKRAINE GIRL NAMES

1. Alona
This Ukrainian name means strong as an Oaktree.

2. Anastasiya
This name is a Russian and Ukrainian version of the Latin name Anastasia. This means resurrection.

3. Angelina
This name has been Derived originally from the Greek language. It means messenger.

4. Anichka
This name refers to a graceful woman. This also means grace.

5. Anna

This name is Of Latin and Greek origins. This name has the meaning of grace or favor.

6. Antonina

A Ukrainian name that means priceless. It is one of the traditional Ukrainian names.

7. Bohdana

This name is a feminine variant of the Czech/ Ukrainian name Bohdan. It means God's gift.

8. Bohuslava

This name is a feminine form of the Czech/ Ukrainian name Bohuslav. It means God's glory.

9. Boyka

It is a feminine version of the Ukrainian name Boyko. It means an inhabitant of western Ukraine.

10. Daniela

This is a feminine form of the Italian name Daniele and Ukrainian name Danilo. It means God is my judge.

11. Daryna
This name is a Ukrainian form of the Roman name Daria. It refers to a gift of God.

12. Galyna
This name means a girl who stays quiet and calm, regardless of the situation. It also means calmness.

13. Ganna
This beautiful name means a woman who is full of grace.

14. Inna
This name is the Ukrainian term for a fast-flowing stream of water.

15. Ionna
This name means a gift of God.

16. Ivanna
This is a Biblical name. It means God is gracious.

17. Kalyna
This is a Ukrainian name derived from the Ukrainian name of a guilder rose plant.

18. Kateryna

This name is a Ukrainian form of the name Katherine. It means pure.

19. Katrya

This name means a pure and chaste woman.

20. Lyudmyla

This name is a Ukrainian variant of the Czech/Russian name Ludmila. It means people's favor.

21. Mariya

This name is perfect for little girls. It means beloved, star of the sea, or loved. It is the Ukrainian form of the name Maria.

22. Maryna

This name is a variant of the name Marina. It refers to one who is of the sea.

23. Mikhaila

This name is a variant of the Ukrainian name Mykhaila. It means one who is like God.

24. Myroslava
A traditional Slavic name meaning 'glorious'. It is pronounced 'mir-oh-slava'.

25. Nataliya
This is a Ukrainian and Russian version of Natalia. It means birthday, or in Church Latin Christmas day.

26. Natalka
This name is a Ukrainian pet form of the name Nataliya. It refers to birthday, or in Church Latin Christmas day.

27. Nina
This lovely traditional name means fish in Ukraine.

28. Oksana
This is a Russian and Ukrainian form of the Greek name Xenia. It means hospitable (especially to foreigners and strangers).

29. Olena
This name is a Ukrainian version of the name Helen. It means orch or moon.

30. Oxana

This is a variant of the Russian/Ukrainian name Oksana. It refers to someone who is hospitable (especially to foreigners and strangers).

31. Polina

This name is Commonly used in Ukrainian, Russian, Greek, and Polish culture. It means humble.

32. Roksolana

It is a beautiful Ukrainian name dating back to the Middle Ages. It means a woman from the Roksolan tribe.

33. Ruslana

This Slavic female name means lioness.

34. Sofiya

This name is a Russian and Ukrainian variant of the Greek name Sophia. It means wisdom.

35. Solomiya

This Ukrainian name is originally derived from the Greek language. It means peace.

36. Svetlana

Svetlana (Russian) or Svitlana (Ukrainian) is a name that means light, bright, pure soul. The shortened variants of this name are Sveta or Lana.

37. Veronika

This name is the Ukrainian form of the name Veronica. It means to bring victory.

38. Vesna

This name is derived from the name of an ancient Slavic Goddess. It refers to Spring.

39. Viktoria

This well-known name means victory.

40. Viktoriya

This is a Russian and Ukrainian variant of the Roman name Victoria. It means to conquer; victory.

41. Vladyslava

This name has strong Slavic roots. It means glory.

42. Wasylyna
This is a feminine version of the Ukrainian name Wasyl. It means king.

43. Xristina
This name has its roots in the Greek language. It refers to a follower of Christ.

44. Yana
This name has Ukrainian and Russian origins. It means gift of God.

45. Yaroslava
It is a traditional name that means glorious and fierce.

46. Yaryna
It is a graceful Ukrainian feminine name that means peaceful. It is pronounced 'yah-rih-nah'.

47. Yelysaveta
This name is The Ukrainian alteration of the name Elisabeth. This beautiful name means devoted to God. The name is pronounced 'ye-liza-viet-uh'.

48. Yeva

This name is the Ukrainian modification of the name Eve. It means life. It is pronounced 'yeh-vah'.

49. Yulia

It is A form of the name Julia. It means youthful.

50. Zlata

This is one of the most popular girl names. Zlata means gold or golden.

"A good name is more desirable than great riches; to be esteemed is better than silver or gold." – Proverbs 22:1 (NIV)

In a world brimming with words, we use language to distinguish, order and associate. Words are likewise used to name, characterize and contrast as we use them to portray ourselves and the individuals around us.

UKRAINE BOYS NAMES

Andriy is a Ukrainian form of Andrew, meaning **man; warrior**.

Bohdan
Bohdan is a Czech and Ukrainian form of Bogdan, meaning **God-gift**.

Bohuslav
Bohuslav is a Czech and Ukrainian form of Polish Boguslaw, meaning **God-Glory**.

Borysko
Borysko is a Ukrainian form of Russian Boris probably meaning **fighter, warrior**.

Boyko

Ukrainian ethnic group name turned surname turned forename. It started with a group of Ukrainian montagnards of the Carpathian highlands; it is from this ethnic group that the surname derived which turned to forename. The name, itself, derived from the word "bojko", meaning **inhabitant of western Ukraine**.

Danylo

Danylo is a Ukrainian form of Daniel, meaning **God is my judge**.

Dmytro

Dmytro is a Ukrainian form of Greek Demetrios, meaning **loves the earth**.

Fedir

Fedir is a Ukrainian form of English Theodore, meaning **gift of God**.

Hedeon

Hedeon is a Ukrainian form of Hebrew Gideon, meaning **hewer; one who cuts trees**.

Hryhoriy

Hryhoriy is a Ukrainian form of English Gregory, meaning **watchful; vigilant.**

Krystiyan

Krystiyan is a Ukrainian form of Christian, meaning **follower of Christ.**

Kyrylo

Kyrylo is a Ukrainian form of English Cyril, meaning **lord.**

Lyaksandro

Lyaksandro is a Ukrainian form of Alexander, meaning **defender of mankind.**

Marko

Marko is a Ukrainian form of Marcus, meaning **warlike.**

Matviy

Matviy is a Ukrainian form of Matthew, meaning **gift of God.**

Mykhailo

Mykhailo is a Ukrainian form of Michael, meaning **who is like God?**

Mykola

Mykola is a Ukrainian form of Nicholas, meaning **victory of the people**.

Olek

Olek is a nickname for Ukrainian Oleksander, meaning **defender of mankind**.

Oleksander

Oleksander is a Ukrainian form of Alexander, meaning **defender of mankind**.

Oleksiy

Oleksiy is a Ukrainian form of Greek Alexius, meaning **defender**.

Pavlo

Pavlo is a Ukrainian form of Paul, meaning **small**.

Petro

Petro is an Esperanto and Ukrainian form of Peter, meaning **rock; stone**.

Petruso

Petruso is a Ukrainian form of Peter, meaning **rock; stone**.

Pylyp

Pylyp is a Ukrainian form of English Philip, meaning **horse lover**.

Symon

Symon is a Ukrainian form of Greek Simon, meaning **hearkening**.

Taras

Taras is a Russian and Ukrainian form of Greek Tarasios, meaning **of Tarentum**.

Vasyl

Vasyl is a Ukrainian form of English Basil, meaning **king**.

Volodymyr

Volodymyr is a Ukrainian form of Slavic Vladimir, meaning **famous ruler**.

Yakiv

Yakiv is a Ukrainian form of Jacob, meaning **supplanter**.

Yevheniy

Yevheniy is a Ukrainian form of Eugene, meaning **well born**.

Yosyp

Yosyp is a Ukrainian form of Joseph, meaning **shall add**, which is usually taken to mean **God will add another son**.

Ukrainian boy wearing national costume

ABOUT THE AUTHOR

AL Katar was born a baby of the Civil Rights Movement in the mid 1950's. A child of the 60's. A man of the 70's and a storyteller of the 21st t century, who hasn't forgotten the great writers of the past. He writes in the action, suspense, drama, comedy and the everyday "just be real with me story" genre. From stories titled "The Last Warrior",

"Gator Restaurant", "Third Strike", "Drop Off Zone", "The Monkey", "Pensacola Sharks", "Meet Black People" just to name a few and also a bonus feature "Education, The Sitcom", Katar consider himself to be a transfer writer. Katar to his knowledge is the only writer to publish a three book trilogy on the black pirate "Captain Scratch". He is looking for representation in the film, book and entertainment industry. Katar hopes to build a meaningful relationship and partner with progressive Hollywood studios to maximize sales of a number of his books to be made into movies. He believes with the right management team and investment network the sky is the limit. Some wise person once said only when a writer is stretched and has suffered, that writer will become better. Katar is ready and willing to suffer and to be stretched all the more. See Amazon/AL katar/ Books.

AL Katar at Work

Credits/Contributors

Education News Network (ENN)

Of Pensacola, Florida

Mr. Cedric (Cid) Langham

ENN Vice President Chicago, Illinois

Publicist

Patricia Ann Pryor

Country Line Music.Com

Song "My Heart" written by AL Pryor

Three Broke Comics.Com

Writing Staff

Scratch Kids Products

Bug Tubes

Spencer For Hire Graphics of Pensacola,

Florida, for front and back cover.

Avonbuynow.com

www.ingramcontent.com/pod-product-compliance
Lightning Source LLC
Chambersburg PA
CBHW071951190726
48293CB00004B/1424